NO LONGER PROPERTY OF
A
RANG

Valentine ABCs

Story and Art by
Patricia Reeder Eubank

ideals children's books.
Nashville, Tennessee

ISBN-13: 978-0-8249-5597-7

Published by Ideals Children's Books
An imprint of Ideals Publications
A Guideposts Company
Nashville, Tennessee
www.idealsbooks.com

Copyright © 2009 by Patricia Reeder Eubank

All rights reserved. No part of this publication may
be reproduced or transmitted in any form or by
any means, electronic or mechanical, including
photocopy, recording, or any information storage
and retrieval system, without permission in
writing from the publisher.

For Winchester, who is the best artist of
knights and castles I know, has such a wonderful
sense of humor and enormous imagination, loves
animals (especially Newfies) so much, is so kind
and caring, and is such an amazing outdoorsman.

Color separations by Precision Color
Graphics, Franklin, Wisconsin
Printed and bound in the U.S.A.

Library of Congress CIP data on file

Designed by Georgina Chidlow-Rucker

10 9 8 7 6 5 4 3 2 1

You can visit Patti Eubank online
at www.patriciaeubank.com

On a cold, wintry night before Valentine's Day, Little Dragon was hard at work in his family's cozy cave. He had lots of friends and family, and he wanted to make a festive valentine for each of them. So he cut and he colored. He drew and he glued. And he made very special hearts from A to Z . . .

A is for ancient Aunt Abigail, with amber scales like armor to touch.

Her Angora cat is adorable, her applesauce cookies awesome to munch.

B is for big brother Brian,
who's burly, brawny,
and brave.

He badgers Black Forest bears
for berries both
dragons do crave.

B

C is for cute Catalina,
the castle's cool calico cat.

She constantly climbs
crenelations,
quite close to the edge,
at that.

CATALINA

D is for Little Dragon's daddy, who travels at a fast pace.

He carries Little Dragon piggyback under drawbridge and over moat space.

DADDY

D

E is for exuberant Emily,
a sheepdog
who loves to explore.

Eagerly she digs for
treasures in the castle's
hard earthen floor.

F is for Frederic, a firedrake
who flies with feisty finesse.

Frequently he eats French fries
while playing long games
of chess.

G is for Grandma and Grandpa,
who love Little Dragon
with all of their might.

They giggle and grin and
play card games whenever
he spends the night.

H is for Henry,
Sir Harold's horse,
who wears helmet and
hardware galore.

He happily plays games
of horseshoes outside the
heavy oak door.

ROYAL MEWS

HENRY

I is for Ivan and Isabelle, inky black twins just learning to fly.

Swooping and swirling in tandem, they're impressive to watch in the sky.

ISABELLE + IVAN

J is for jumping Jeremy,
the court jester, a jovial fellow.

He can jabber and juggle
ten jackfruit: juicy,
jade green, and yellow.

J

K is for kindly King Kendrick,
busy with knights
and knaves.

Sometimes he and his kestrel
sneak off to fish the blue waves.

L is for lovable Ludwig,
a lion with a loud roar.

He likes to scare
ladies in waiting,
then nap with a
lyrical snore.

LUDWIG

L

M is for Little Dragon's mama,
who loves to plant flowers
and cook.

Each evening she gathers
her dragons to snuggle and
read them a book.

N is for neighbor Nolina,
a Newfie, so nurturing and big.

Each night she nestles
her noisy pups
in nighthawk feathers
and twigs.

O is for Oscar, an owl friend,
who lives in an old oak tree.

He flies under opalescent
moonlight, his outline
so easy to see.

P is for Princess Penelope,
who's partial to pizza
and puppies.

Although she loves stomping
through puddles,
she's pretty and proper
to see.

P

Q is for quiet Queen Quella,
who quilts and cooks royal treats.

Little Dragon's favorites are
Quince jam, quick breads,
and savory mincemeat.

R is for red-haired Rusulka,
a mermaid
from under the sea.

She rollicks in rolling waters
and finds trinkets
she shares readily.

R

S is for Samantha and Savannah,
who are sassy, silly, and sweet.

Little Dragon's siblings
share secrets, swap stuffies,
and play hide-and-seek.

T is for three-headed Mr. Teasdale,
a teacher with a tail tan and red.

He teaches reading, writing,
and 'rithmetic,
one subject with each head.

U is for unique Auntie Ulma,
a unicorn kind but untamed.

She studies the stars in the universe
and knows constellations
by name.

V is for valiant old Victor,
a dragon who lives near the moat.

Many Vikings have carved
his visage on the fronts
of their very long boats.

W is for wise old Winchester,
a wizard with
white trailing beard.

Little Dragon and he often
wander the woodlands
without any fear.

X is for expert Sir Xebic,
Little Dragon's
favorite knight.

Little Dragon likes
to examine his armor,
all shiny and bright.

Y is for young yeoman Yousef,
who tends to his yarrow
each day.

He yodels and yokes up
his oxen, then loads up
his wagon with hay.

YOUSEF

Z is for Great-Grandma Zinny,
zooming through life
with great zest.

She plays zany songs
on her zither, her talent
above all the rest.

Z

GREAT
GRAND
ZINNY

W hen Little Dragon finished, his eyes were drooping and he yawned widely. Mama Dragon scooped him up and snuggled him into bed. Near the foot of the bed sat the basket of hearts he had created. Soon Little Dragon drifted off to sleep, dreaming of the valentines he would share with his friends and family.